T0047181

To:

_____

From:

_____

Date:

_____

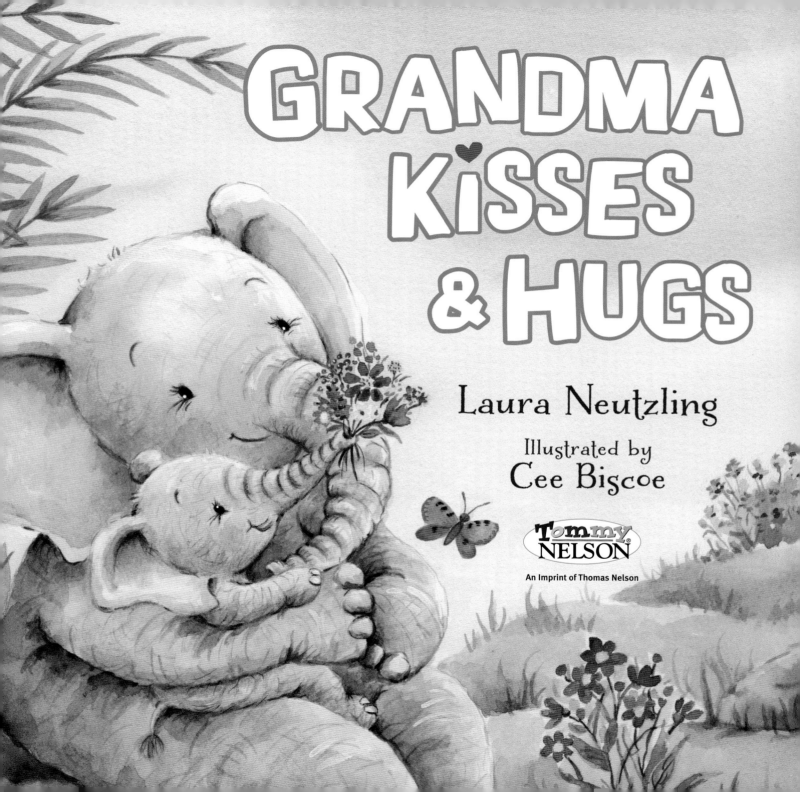

GRANDMA KISSES & HUGS

Laura Neutzling

Illustrated by
Cee Biscoe

Tommy
NELSON®

An Imprint of Thomas Nelson

Grandma Kisses and Hugs

© 2021 Thomas Nelson

Tommy Nelson, PO Box 141000, Nashville, TN 37214

Portions of this book were previously published as *Grandma Kisses*.

All rights reserved. No portion of this book may be reproduced, stored in a retrieval system, or transmitted in any form or by any means—electronic, mechanical, photocopy, recording, scanning, or other—except for brief quotations in critical reviews or articles, without the prior written permission of the publisher.

Published in Nashville, Tennessee, by Tommy Nelson. Tommy Nelson is an imprint of Thomas Nelson. Thomas Nelson is a registered trademark of HarperCollins Christian Publishing, Inc.

Tommy Nelson titles may be purchased in bulk for educational, business, fund-raising, or sales promotional use. For information, please e-mail SpecialMarkets@ThomasNelson.com.

Scripture quotations are taken from the International Children's Bible®. Copyright © 1986, 1988, 1999, 2015 by Thomas Nelson. Used by permission. All rights reserved.

ISBN 978-1-4002-2374-9 (eBook)

Library of Congress Cataloging-in-Publication Data

Names: Neutzling, Laura, author. | Stapler, Suzanna, author. | Biscoe, Cee, illustrator.
Title: Grandma kisses and hugs / Laura Neutzling ; with Suzanna Stapler ; illustrated by Cee Biscoe.
Description: Nashville, Tennessee : Tommmy Nelson, [2021] | Audience: Ages 4-8. | Summary: "Celebrates the joys of being with Grandma, from baking cookies to reading Bible stories together to snuggling before bed!"-- Provided by publisher.
Identifiers: LCCN 2020025717 (print) | LCCN 2020025718 (ebook) | ISBN 9781400223756 (hardcover) | ISBN 9781400223749 (epub)
Subjects: CYAC: Stories in rhyme. | Grandmothers--Fiction. | Animals--Fiction. | Christian life--Fiction.
Classification: LCC PZ8.3.N3694 Grd 2021 (print) | LCC PZ8.3.N3694 (ebook) | DDC [E]--dc23
LC record available at https://lccn.loc.gov/2020025717
LC ebook record available at https://lccn.loc.gov/2020025718

ISBN 978-1-4002-2375-6

Written by Laura Neutzling and Suzanna Stapler

Illustrated by Cee Biscoe

Printed in China

21 22 23 24 25 DSC 6 5 4 3 2 1

Mfr: DSC / Dongguan, China / February 2021 / PO #9589881

We love because God first loved us.

—1 John 4:19

Grandma's kisses on my face
Could not be any bigger!
But I don't mind—I just know
I'm happy when I'm with her.

Kiss, kiss, kiss. I love a Grandma kiss!

Grandma's hugs are full of love,
Although a wee bit tight.
She wraps her arms around me,
Squeezing with all her might.

Grandma time is just so great.
She loves to share her things.
She lets me wear her nicest hat
And pushes when I swing.

Grandma's walks are extra fun.
We **play** and **romp** and **roam**.
When we've finished counting trees,
We finally turn back home!

Walk, walk, walk. I love a Grandma walk!

Grandma's porch is where we sit
And watch the clouds go by.
We point to all the funny shapes
That float across the sky!

Grandma crafts with paint and glue.
We sometimes make a mess.
But when we've finished working hard,
It feels so great to rest!

Grandma's books explore the world.
We read them to each other.
Page by page, she makes it fun—
I hope we read another!

Book, book, book. I love a Grandma book!

Grandma's sweaters smell like spring.
She knits them each by hand.
Colors, dots, and **sparkly stripes**—
The one I pick looks grand!

Grandma's games bring many smiles.
My favorite's hide-and-seek.
Every time she finds me,
She gives a happy squeak!

Grandma's laugh is big and loud
When we joke and play.
Making lots of silly faces,
We could laugh all day.

Giggle, giggle, giggle. I love a Grandma giggle!

Grandma's flowers grow so bright—
Pink, yellow, red, and blue.
I pick the ones that she likes best
And tell her, "I love you!"

Grandma's lap is **safe and warm**,
Rocking as we read
The stories from her Bible,
Of God's great love for me!

Grandma's cookies taste so good.
They're soft and warm and yummy.
No one bakes like Grandma does.
I want them in my tummy!

Cookie, cookie, cookie. I love a Grandma cookie!

Grandma's ears will listen close
When I get scared or sad.
I know she's always there to help,
So things don't seem so bad.

Grandma's songs ring bright and clear
And have a happy beat.
We dance and spin around the room
Until the tune's complete.

Song, song, song. I love a Grandma song!

Grandma's eyes sparkle and shine
As we gaze at stars and trees.
It's good to know in this big world
She's looking out for me.

Grandma's prayers are strong and sweet
While tucking me in tight.
"God, please watch my little one,
And keep us through the night."

Grandma's kisses come once more
As we turn off the lights.
She says, "Sweet dreams! I love you so."
I yawn, "You too. Goodnight!"

Kiss, kiss, kiss. I love a Grandma kiss!

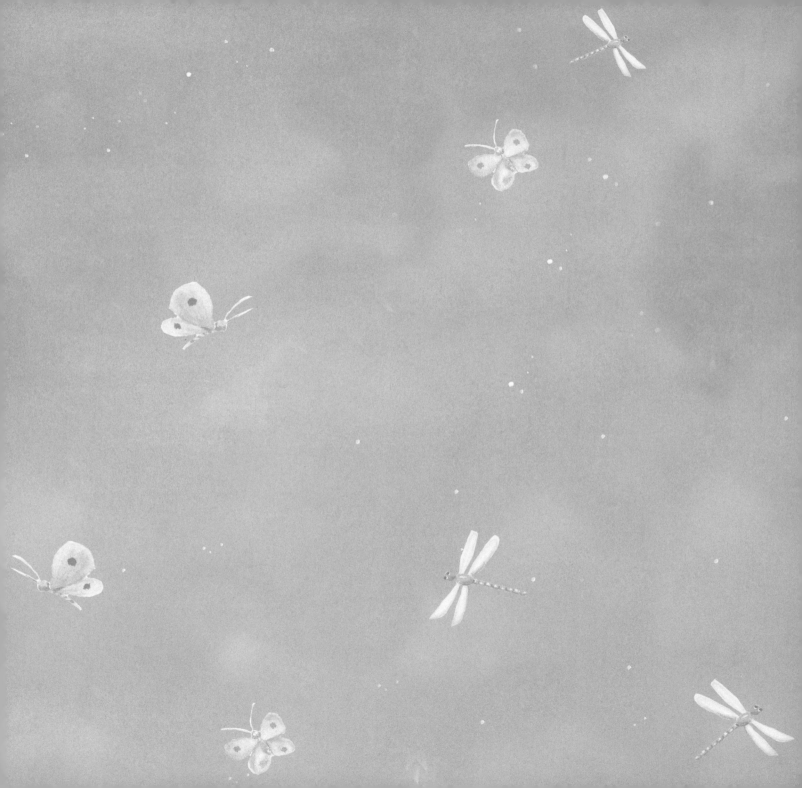